D1064936

The Orphan & the Qallupilluit

The Nunavummi reading series is a Nunavut-developed levelled book series that supports literacy development while teaching readers about the people, traditions, and environment of the Canadian Arctic.

Published in Canada by Nunavummi, an imprint of Inhabit Education Books Inc. | www.inhabiteducation.com

Inhabit Education Books Inc.
(Iqaluit) P.O. Box 2129, Iqaluit, Nunavut, X0A 1H0
(Toronto) 191 Eglinton Avenue East, Suite 301, Toronto, Ontario, M4P 1K1

Printed in Canada.

Library and Archives Canada Cataloguing in Publication

Title: The orphan & the Qallupilluit / written by Neil Christopher ; illustrated by Jim Nelson.
Other titles: Orphan and the Qallupilluit
Names: Christopher, Neil, 1972- author. | Nelson, Jim, 1962- illustrator.
Description: Series statement: Nunavummi reading series
Identifiers: Canadiana 20190199407 | ISBN 9780228704850 (hardcover)
Classification: LCC PS8605.H754 O77 2020 | DDC jC813/.6—dc23

ISBN: 978-0-2287-0485-0

The Orphan & the Qallupilluit

WRITTEN BY

Neil Christopher

ILLUSTRATED BY

Jim Nelson

Long ago, there was an orphan who had proven his courage and wisdom by saving the other children in his camp from a large and scary ogress. This had earned him the respect and friendship of the other children.

But this orphan still felt lonely, as he had no family at the camp. No one invited the orphan into their tents. No one asked the orphan to eat with their families.

When the children went inside for the night, the orphan had to stay outside alone.

"Everyone needs a home! I will find a home for myself," the orphan decided.

So, the next morning, he packed up all that he owned, which was not very much.

Then he left the camp and walked out onto the land, looking for adventure and a home.

The orphan walked and walked. After a day of walking, he was beyond any landmarks he recognized.

Eventually, he could smell the salt in the air. He knew he must be close to the sea. He stopped and listened carefully. He could hear seabirds squawking.

The orphan ran up a hill and saw the ocean in the distance. It was almost the end of spring. The snow was almost completely gone from the land, but the sea was still covered with broken ice.

The orphan ran down the hill toward the sea. He was hungry and hoping to find some food.

The orphan walked out onto the ice and looked for a wide crack that he could fish in. He quickly found a good place to fish and pulled out his hook and line.

It wasn't long before he caught his first codfish. It was big and difficult to get onto the ice.

"It seems I am a great fisherman," the orphan said to the seagull that had been watching him. **"This will be the best meal I have had in a long time!"**

"That's what we were thinking as well," said a strange voice from behind him.

The orphan froze with fear.

Slowly, the orphan turned around to see three strange creatures crawling out of an ice crack.

These creatures looked like nothing he had ever seen before. Their skin was scaly, like a fish. Their hands were large and webbed. They all wore large jackets made of feathers.

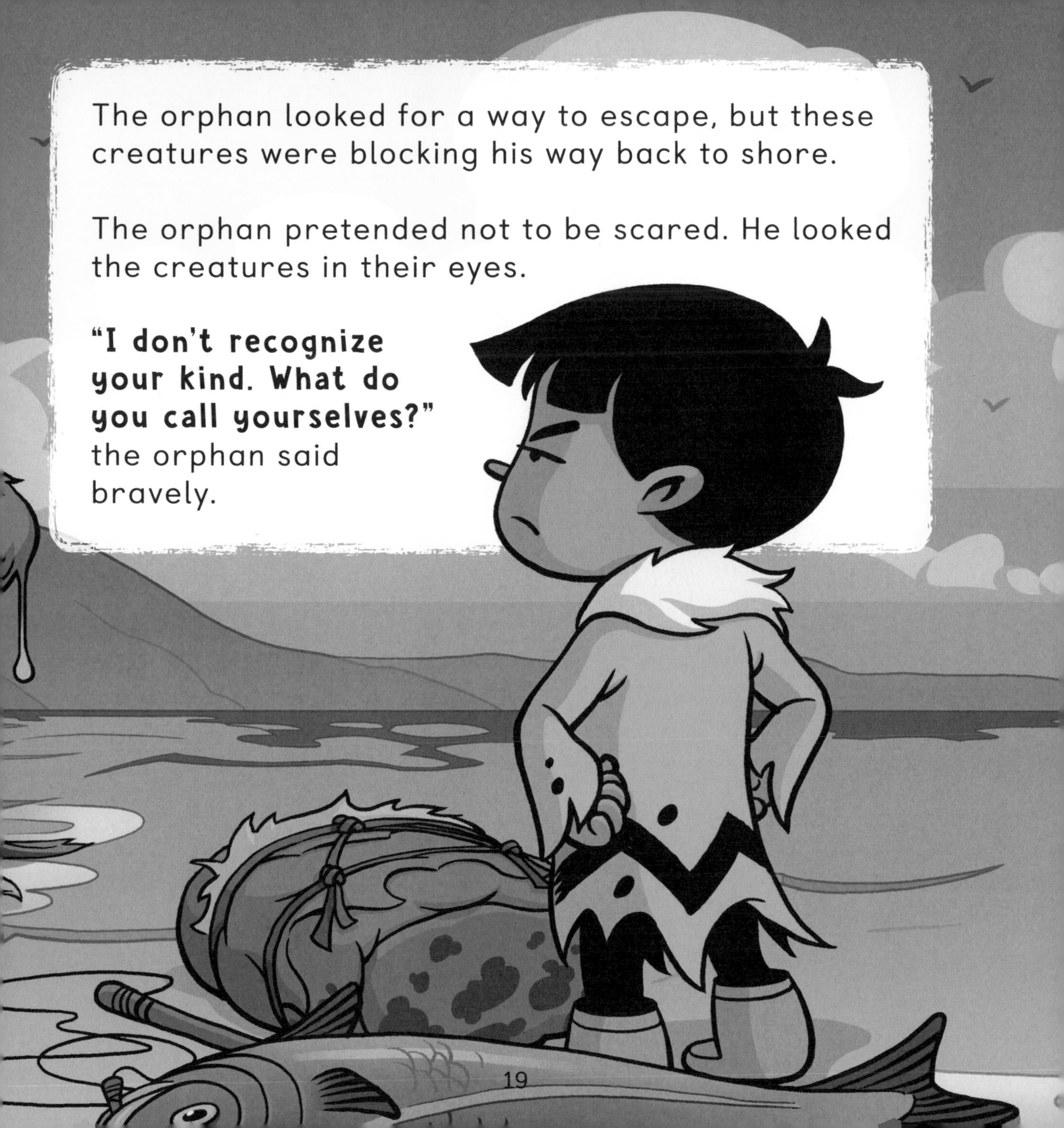

The orphan looked for a way to escape, but these creatures were blocking his way back to shore.

The orphan pretended not to be scared. He looked the creatures in their eyes.

"I don't recognize your kind. What do you call yourselves?" the orphan said bravely.

The creatures looked at each other. They had never known a child to speak to them so confidently.

"We are the *qallupilluit*,"* said the first creature.

"We live under the water, waiting for silly children to come play on the broken ice," said the second.

"Silly children like you!" said the third.

***qallupilluit** (pronounced QAL-lu-PIL-lu-it): mythological sea creatures that steal children through ice cracks

"**Qallupilluit,**" said the orphan to himself. He had heard Elders telling stories of these creatures. He remembered some things from those stories.

He remembered that the creatures could not come onto the land because they hated lichen.

He also remembered that they were greedy.

The orphan smiled and said, **"I know where there are a lot of silly children."**

The qallupilluit looked at each other excitedly.

"Where are these children?" said the first creature.

"Yes, we would like to meet them!" said the second.

"Let me take you to them," said the orphan. He picked up his codfish and started walking toward shore.

The qallupilluit were so excited that they let the orphan walk past them, and they followed behind.

"Where are the children?" asked the third creature.

"Just over the hill," the orphan answered.

But when the orphan got to the shore, he turned around and smiled at the three creatures.

"I remember hearing a story about qallupilluit. Is it true that you don't like lichen?" the orphan asked.

"We hate lichen! It sticks to our skin. That is why we cannot come onto the beach," hissed the first creature.

"That is what I thought!" said the orphan.

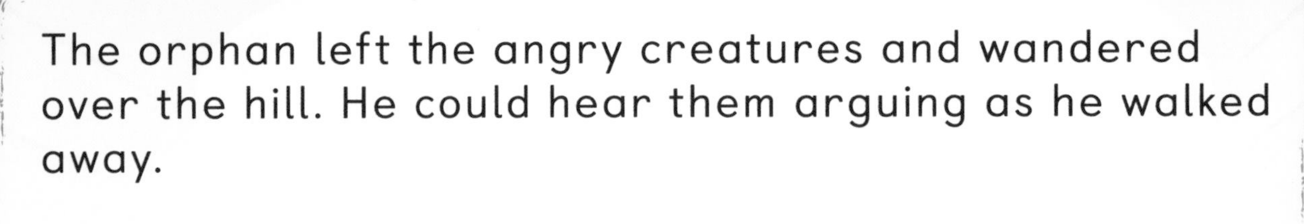

The orphan left the angry creatures and wandered over the hill. He could hear them arguing as he walked away.

The orphan ate his fat fish. He was ready for another adventure.

He continued on his journey to find a home.

Inuktitut Glossary

Notes on Inuktitut pronunciation: There are some sounds in Inuktitut that may be unfamiliar to English speakers. The pronunciations below convey those sounds in the following ways:

- Capitalized letters indicate the emphasis.
- **q** is a "uvular" sound, which is a sound that comes from the very back of the throat (the uvula). This is different from the **k** sound, which is the same as the typical English **k** sound.
- ll is a rolled "l" sound.

qallupilluit QAL-lu-PIL-lu-it	**mythological sea creatures that steal children through ice cracks**

For more Inuktitut pronunciation resources, please visit inhabiteducation.com/inuitnipingit.

Nunavummi
Reading Series

The Nunavummi reading series is a Nunavut-developed levelled book series that supports literacy development while teaching readers about the people, traditions, and environment of the Canadian Arctic.

- 16–32 pages
- Sentences and stories become longer and more complex
- Varied punctuation
- Dialogue is included in fiction texts
- Readers rely more on the words than the images to decode the text

- 24–32 pages
- Sentences become complex and varied
- Varied punctuation
- Dialogue is included in fiction texts and is necessary to understand the story
- Readers rely more on the words than the images to decode the text

- 24–40 pages
- Sentences are complex and vary in length
- Lots of varied punctuation
- Dialogue is included in fiction texts and is necessary to understand the story
- Readers rely on the words to decode the text; images are present but only somewhat supportive

Fountas & Pinnell Text Level: L

This book has been officially levelled using the F&P Text Level Gradient™ Leveling System.

Nunavummi